Darkest Kink

© 2019 The Secret Submissive. All rights reserved.

Stifle fear and rouse your deepest desires.
Carve a playground in which to feed your curiosity
and simply take the plunge.

About the Author

Nisha's story explores the wild yearning and choked desires of a Submissive who desperately craves a firmer, and altogether darker, taste of submission. As the third instalment in the series, this tale represents so much of where I am now in my journey, two and a half years after my very first BDSM session with my adored Dom (check out my first story, *The Good Indian Girl.*)

It's impossible to pinpoint exactly when it happened but it was a significant moment for me when I recognised that I genuinely trusted Sir, wholly and completely. As I wrote *Darkest Kink*, I enjoyed the fact that Nisha's thoughts and feelings starkly contrasted with those of Leni in *The Good Indian Girl*. So many of the fears and insecurities I had felt during those early days of exploration had somehow - and somewhere along the way - just melted into insignificance. Sir had built trust between us with his kindness, patience and care, and it marked the way for us to enjoy rougher, firmer, filthier sessions, and to bring to life some of our naughtier desires. One of the most exciting parts of the last year has definitely been sharing and exploring new fantasies with Sir, and with each session, pushing our experiences to dizzying new heights.

Darkest Kink follows an experienced submissive as she tentatively reveals, to her dominant, her desire for consensual non-consent play. Nisha thrives on the pleasure of being pinned under Sir's strong body with nowhere to run; she aches to relinquish every ounce of control and to submit completely to her master. As her dominant sets the wheels in motion and brings her most depraved vision to life, how will the reality of receiving such brutal treatment compare to the clit-trembling, debauched fantasy which she has longed for but resisted for so many years?

Nisha's Taste of Submission: Darkest Kink

You have reached your destination. I pulled forward, through a shrouded arch of burnt orange and auburn leaves, crunching sand and gravel beneath my tyres. A wave of nausea washed over me as I slipped down into first gear and scanned the towering hedges around the perimeter of the secluded carpark. Pulling slowly into a parking space, I turned the key in the ignition; light and sound drained, throwing an eerie stillness into the space around me. I glanced around; shadows danced in far corners, toying and twisting with my desires. I was early but I wondered if he was early too - watching and waiting. My eyes climbed the thick trunk of the old oak tree that stood at the far side of the disused carpark. I continued along the branches, to the spindly tips, and the silver crescent of the moon appeared from behind a smudge of cloud, casting a cool light over the bonnet of my car. Ahead of me, three black and yellow bollards blocked the exit, leaving only one way in and only one way out. There was no backing out now.

Leaning over to the passenger side, I prepared my overnight bag, as per his request: handbag inside and phone on silent, making sure everything was fully zipped and tightly secured. Just the way he likes me – a smirk spread across my face in response to the fleeting thought -tightly secured with nowhere to run and nowhere to hide. My entire body clenched and ached with nerves. I wanted to text him, so desperately – I knew he would calm me down in a heartbeat but we had decided on zero contact. Maybe I should ring Aarav instead? I wondered. I loved my husband to pieces but if I called him now then I would have to explain myself. He wouldn't understand and then he would spend all weekend worrying; I couldn't do that to him. I had to be brave.

I tried sifting my nerves into rationality but it was no use – my stomach was twisting and knotting. I needed air. Throwing open the driver's door, I gulped down mouthfuls of cool autumn air and let the breeze caress my bare arms and legs, in an attempt to calm myself down. The sound of my heartbeat emanated from my chest, thudding with vivacity. I swivelled my legs to the side, nervously jostling them and digging the stiletto heels of my black-suede sandals into the dust. I tugged a frayed thread on the hem of my denim skirt, tiptoeing and tensing my calves. My eyes scanned up and down my body – thighs, torso, and forearms. Had it not been for the beauty-spot that sat half-way up the outer edge of my left thigh, I could have sworn I was in somebody else's body. How could Nisha Chaudhary - wife, mother, discerning solicitor - have made it this far down the road of submission?

Removing the keys from the ignition slot, I toyed with the dangling red Om keyring, rotating it between my thumb and forefinger. I thought back to last Diwali when Diya had given it to me – I wondered what she would be doing right now – whether Aarav would have managed to get her to sleep by now or whether she would be running rings around him. I wondered if he would have given her the bhinda nu shaak and rotlis I cooked this afternoon, or whether he would have ordered pizza - definitely pizza. A nubbin of guilt tried to sprout from my thoughts but I suppressed it. Compartmentalising my life was the only way to make this work. I kissed my family goodnight, leaving Nisha - wife and mother - firmly behind. Nisha - the cock-hungry, obedient submissive - was more than ready to come out to play and I had to let her.

Pulling the black and white striped holdall over the gearstick, I slipped out of the car and locked it, zipping my keys away before dumping the bag on the bonnet. I had over twenty minutes left to kill – time was dragging its heels and it was making me needier than ever. Glancing around the entirety of the deserted car park, three times, I was confident it was empty. The sweet scent of my wet, sticky cunt captured my attention, luring my fingers up my skirt towards my white cotton knickers. He always loved the taste of my arousal smeared across my fingers; plus, I was alone so why not? I leaned against the side of the car and closed my eyes lightly, concentrating on the contrasting sensation of heat radiating from between my thighs and the breeze that pulled the hairs on my arms to attention. I focused on the powdery softness of the thin skin between my legs, gathering the gusset of my knickers to one slide and sliding my fingers against the puffy warmth of my cunt-lips. An unexpected moan slipped from my lips as I opened myself slightly with two fingers, coating myself in my own clear nectar. I imagined his fingers in place of mine, wider and rougher, as I moved them over my swollen, throbbing clit. With each long, tantalising stroke, my fears melted into desire, fuelling a succession of rapid, circular movements around my needy bud. I parted my thighs further, desperate for better access. Imagining all of the wonders that the night had in store for me, I felt my mind whip away from reality in a frenzy of hope and excitement. At that moment, I didn't care an ounce for the rules; I just needed to cum.

"Whore..." The growl of that single word tore through my ecstasy and pulled me back to the menacing darkness around me; the moon was veiled behind a mantle of sombre, slate-grey cloud. I yelled out with all my might and whipped my head towards the imperious voice; however, I heard nothing but a whimper leave my body and saw nothing but a flash of black sleeve. Smothered and stifled - my scream wrestled against the leather-bound hand that clamped so completely over my mouth. His thick fingers clenched around my waist, holding me against his body as he lifted me with ease. My knickers sat uncomfortably, wedged between my lips, and my heels scraped piercingly through the dirt ground as he dragged me away from my car.

My screams were more sincere than I had ever anticipated - the cold leather of his jacket and gloves was more intimidating than I had expected. He didn't look anything like Sir; he didn't feel like Sir, and he didn't smell like him either. As though somebody had hit fast-forward, my thoughts raced ahead of any form of rationality, looping and tangling like a jarred reel.

He was early – too early?

Bile rose in my throat as a sickening thought bloomed: what if it wasn't him? I thrashed as he yanked open the back doors of a white van and thrust me towards it like a stray animal, ready to be impounded. Wavering on the fine point of my scuffed heels, my legs shook as he grasped the back of my neck and forced me to kneel – the base of the van was hard and uncomfortable against the protruding bones of my shins and knees.

"Quiet," he hissed the threat directly into my ear, locking my body to the spot. I tried to play his voice back to myself but there wasn't enough for me to decipher whether or not it was Sir speaking. Tears of sheer panic and frustration began to well on my lower lash line. A cold sweat coated my back and my bottom lip began to shake involuntarily. I felt a soft, thick cloth push into my mouth – dry against my tongue – and fill me until my whimpers were silenced; tape wrapped and wrapped around my head, securing it firmly in place.

Desperately clinging on to any sense of control, erratically, I scanned the interior of the van that would imminently become my holding pen. Although it was dark, I could just about see that it had been completely gutted - just three seats remained, facing towards the rear. There was nothing there that would help me. A blindfold came down over my eyes and plunged me into enigmatic darkness. With a bump, he flipped me from my knees onto my arse, half dragging and half carrying me deeper into the confinement of the van. The echoing clout of his heavy footsteps, together with the sound of my dragging body, infiltrated my senses and increased the pace of my punching heart. He used a fistful of my diaphanous blouse to haul me into the seat – I heard a small tear and the rattle of a button hitting the floor and rolling free beneath me. I couldn't just accept whatever bullshit, karmic fate the universe had doled out to me – I was stronger than that. I could still escape. I kicked my leg out, catching him. Where? I didn't know. I followed up my attempted attack with a feeble, blind punch. My knuckles stung and ached. With one hand, he scooped up my wrists and moved forward, trapping my flailing legs between his knees.

"Easy, baby-" A familiar laugh caressed my panic-stricken mind, steadying my heartbeat. He placed his hand on my heart and whispered softly, telling me I was okay.

Sir.

He released my hands and I moved to immediately find his fingers, locking them together with mine and squeezing tightly. I felt burning hot tears of relief seep into the blindfold. I was so grateful for it; I was so grateful that Sir wouldn't see me crying.

"Do you want to continue, Sub? Nod if you do." I paused. Did I want to continue? My tumultuous thoughts settled back to lucidity. Now I knew it was Sir, I felt safe again. I smiled around my gag and nodded, nuzzling against his chest as he attentively fastened and tightened my seatbelt. "As long as you're sure. Good girl." He kissed my forehead before binding my wrists and ankles with thick Velcro straps, making no apologies as he wrenched them taut. As he jumped out of the van and made it jostle, fiery anticipation began to burn steadily in the pit of my stomach once again. "Cause any trouble back there and you'll regret it, girl." He growled, slipping back into character as he slammed the door shut. My clit trembled.

Enveloped in darkness, with just my sweetly depraved thoughts for company, I entertained all of the delicious possibilities that the night held in store for me. I contemplated the utter terror I had just experienced and I thanked God that I was in Sir's hands; I couldn't feel more secure now. Squirming in my ties, I loved how tightly he had bound me. I imagined being trussed up beneath the strength of his body; I played out the first stinging crack of the strap against my arse. My cunt tightened and dampened my knickers as I pictured Sir tethering my wrists to his bed and fucking me until I was a writhing, exhausted mess.

Every sharp turn and firm application of the brakes sent sensual vibrations rippling across every inch of my hyper-sensitive body. I couldn't believe he was bringing my darkest wishes to fruition. From what had started life as a fleck of choked down longing, he had carved a reality that would stay with me forever. My thoughts drifted back to the night he had forced the words from my lips – the night he had coaxed and extracted the sleeping truth from my dormant desires. I knew that tonight would change our relationship forever. I was about to relinquish control further than we had ever played before; I was ready to deepen my submission to him.

***

I loved the way he devoured me with his eyes in public - hungrily and possessively. I smiled back at him with utter adoration as I precariously carried another round of drinks back to our concealed booth in the corner of the bar. My eyes were glassy and a mellow buzz suspended all important thoughts, momentarily. Typically, I would have stopped at this stage but I knew

Sir would get me home safely so another drink wouldn't hurt. I loved being so carefree.

"You're being naughty, Sub – I see what you're doing..." I continued to dig my teeth into the shaft of the straw, a smirk escaping from the corners of my mouth. I shuffled closer to Sir until my thigh touched his and he placed his arm around my body, squeezing tightly. It still felt strange, being out with a man who wasn't my husband – being touched and kissed and caressed by somebody else. Although Aarav understood my need for submission, my craving for kink, it was a desire he just could not satisfy. We dabbled in bondage at first but quickly learned that he just wasn't dominant and he certainly wasn't a sadist, and that was okay. As I slowly revealed the extent of my needs and desires, he eventually suggested that I should find a dominant to see regularly and openly. I fought against the idea for so long – I couldn't do it to him – but I could only run away from myself for so long. Submission was an innate part of me.

I pushed Sir's hand up my inner thigh until the thin material of my navy dress gathered at my crotch. His fingertips dug into and grazed my delicate skin, teasing me wetter and wetter. As instructed, I hadn't worn underwear tonight and I so desperately wished for him to touch my smooth pussy lips and tug the soft curls on my pubic mound. "Tell me what you want, Sub – use your words." He pulled my head back by my hair and lay a deep kiss upon my trembling lips.

"I want to be fucked, Sir. I want to be punished hard for teasing your cock all night…" I whimpered pathetically, unable to lean any closer for a second kiss as he held me firmly in place. He smirked down at me and slapped my thighs apart, running a single finger from my sticky hole to my needy clit. I glanced around the bar, relieved to see that we were adequately concealed.

"You're a good girl. Finish your drink and I'll bundle you into a taxi then." He offered his coated finger to my hungry mouth and I licked and sucked it clean, without any hesitation.

"Do you like the thought of fucking me when I'm tipsy, Sir?" I sucked on the straw, watching the glass empty by half and feeling my head cloud, pleasantly. "I do, Sir," I said with a sinful glaze over my eyes.

"Yes, Sub. Although, either way, I'm going to have you gagged, bound and secured, within the hour. You're all mine tonight – no escaping." He must have felt my cunt tighten and tremble with pleasure at that thought. I felt as though it was written all over my face.

"I love that thought, Sir, so much more than you can even imagine." My mind began to spin into overdrive at the thought of being Sir's personal fuck-toy for the evening. I sucked up the remainder of my drink in a few large gulps, imagining the pleasure, from being restrained tightly and fucked hard, that awaited me. "I'm ready – let's go, Sir!" I slurred, shuffling out of the booth, not a thought given to the rising hem on my short dress.

"Mmm, I love it when you're this needy. You're really feeling the idea of being helplessly bound tonight, aren't you Sub?" He pressed me against the wall and kissed me fully, tongue darting against mine. Pulling down my dress and preserving my modesty for a little while longer, he nodded towards the exit.

"Yes, Sir… completely helpless and at your mercy." My cheeks felt as though they were on fire – I didn't know if I was blushing or just drunk. "Just take me and tie me up, Sir." With alcohol-fuelled audacity, I squeezed the bulge in Sir's trousers.

"If you're not careful, I'll tie you to the spare bed all weekend!" he slapped my arse before putting out his arm for me and guiding me through the crowd. I floated aimlessly in my own thoughts – tossing around my darkest desires as we left the bar. The cold evening air blustered around me and I welcomed Sir's jacket as he draped it over my bare shoulders, guiding me towards the queue of taxis. "Tell me what you're thinking, Sub."

"Nothing, Sir…" I tried to swat away the wicked notions but they bounced back to the forefront of my mind.

"You're forgetting, Sub - I know you." He flagged down a taxi and opened the door for me. "Tell me," he commanded, gently coaxing out the stubborn words.

"I really love being tied up under you, Sir. I love being blindfolded… not knowing what's going to happen next." He knew all that already but I couldn't find the words to share what I really wanted to say. He smiled and fastened my seatbelt, stroking the strap as it nestled between my ample breasts.

"And?" I hated the way he knew me so completely. He glanced over to the rear-view mirror before sliding his hand under my dress, just slightly. He stroked my thigh, soothingly, seeing the effect of that final mojito starting to kick in. "You like the idea of being at my mercy, Sub? Don't you?" He kissed my neck and made me shudder… "So do I."

"I love the thought. I crave it, Sir." I leaned my head back against the rest and closed my eyes. White rum coursed through my veins, making my cunt pulse and throb with longing and excitement. "Sometimes, when you tie me to the headboard and blindfold me, I imagine that you're a stranger… I imagine I don't have a clue what's about to happen." He pushed higher up my thigh, edging me closer. "I love the idea of being your pretty little virgin fuck-toy, Sir." My hand moved to join his – I didn't care if I had an audience. "I love the thought of you making me behave for you, Sir. Taking a sweet and innocent girl and turning her into your filthy little sex-slave." I thrust his fingers very slightly between my lips, sucking air between my teeth as I longed for more. The car jerked as the driver braked harshly, ejecting me abruptly from my perverse fantasy.

Shit.

Did I actually just say that? I opened my eyes and sheepishly withdrew my wandering fingers. I couldn't look at him.

"We definitely need to talk about this when you're sober, Sub," he taunted me, lifting my chin so my eyes were forced to connect with his – he was forcing me to claim my desires. I explored his features, looking for shock or disgust in his reaction. He stroked my cheek with the pad of his thumb, exposing only a glimmer of sadistic intrigue which appeared to rival my own. I bit my lip, coyly, responding with an absence of words. It was clear that things were about to get very interesting.

***

The van lunged to a final stop. Silence. I heard the doors rattle and slam a few times and I wondered what he was doing. It felt like he had been gone for the longest time – he wouldn't leave me all night, would he? The panicked thoughts tried to resurface but I remained in control this time – we'd planned every detail together and we had decided on no curveballs. It was the only way it could work, realistically. I had to trust him – I did trust him. The house alarm sounded, only briefly, which meant that he would be coming for me, imminently. I strained my ears, listening for clues in the inaudible shuffles and scrapes that surrounded me.

The doors flew open and a gust swept over my tied ankles. He didn't speak immediately and I wondered if he was watching me until I heard the faint sound of a car passing. The van dipped as he climbed in and approached me. "Wake the neighbours and you'll be sorry… clear?" he whispered, stroking my cheek. I whipped my head left and then right, in protest, until he muted me with a moderately firm slap across my cheek. "Did I make myself fucking clear?" he repeated, squeezing my jaw. I nodded fervently, pressing my body back into the seat. He unbuckled my belt and dragged me towards the cool, open-air before throwing a hood over my head which only added to my discomfort. He hauled me over his shoulder and slammed the doors closed.

I was surprised at how easily he could carry me. I wondered if I felt heavy to him – after all, I wasn't as slim as I used to be, in my twenties. We hadn't taken more than a few steps when I felt him release one arm from around my body and unlatch the gate. Clever – he must have reversed into the driveway so he could slip me in through the side door and out of sight! I loved the fact that he had thought of every detail – it was more thrilling than I ever could have imagined. The gate swung with a familiar creak, bouncing and tinkling like a wind-chime, as he didn't quite manage to close it fully. He grasped me firmly even when I kicked, writhed and tested his hold. With his free hand, he swatted my uncovered thighs until I gave up in frustration and remained limp.

He carried me up the stairs but he didn't turn right, towards his bedroom. I wondered if being gagged, blindfolded and held upside-down had disorientated me but either way, I just couldn't figure it out. He kicked open the door and stood me on my feet – it took a second for me to steady myself but he held me carefully. I blinked and whimpered as he removed the hood with one, sharp tug and then pulled off my blindfold. The instant relief from the stifling humidity deflated my tensed shoulders and allowed my lungs to fill to maximum capacity. Tossing the hood and blindfold to the floor, he lifted me and threw me onto the mattress in the corner before leaving the room but keeping the door slightly ajar.

Lying on my arm, I flailed like a fish out of water. Shaking away the matted strands of hair that obscured my vision, I allowed my eyes to adjust to the dim yellow light around me. The lampshade had been removed so the bulb was exposed. It swayed, just fractionally, hanging from the ceiling by a thick white wire, casting waving shadows on the cream walls. I scrunched and batted away the hazy black clouds that danced in front of me after being in the dark for so long, taking in my surroundings. The windows were concealed with heavy, black fully-drawn curtains and there was an absence of furniture, aside from the mattress on which he had placed me. It looks like the spare room but it's so completely different, bare like this. I wondered where he had moved the bed, desk and the chest of drawers to. A small webcam sat on one of the shelves opposite me. I smiled at the thought that he would be watching me at all times – I felt more at ease, knowing I would be physically safe.

Before I had the chance to process anything else - to appreciate that feeling of security - he returned. Slamming the door behind him with a reverberating thud, he twisted the key in the lock before zipping it inside his jacket pocket; he patted it, taunting me. The ease I had felt shrank away and disappeared. I swallowed hard, eyes travelling up from the thick tread of his dirt-caked boots, to the wide stance of his muscular thighs, to his broad shoulders and masked face. The addition of a balaclava was unexpected and deliciously menacing! The scowl behind his eyes made my cunt squeeze and throb in anticipation. I wriggled and shuffled back as he approached me, edging and edging until I found the wall behind me.

I looked around and tried to scream for help; the gag was soaked with saliva and did well to muffle my cries. My denim skirt was nearly around my waist and the top four buttons on my blouse had come undone, revealing the left cup of my white cotton bra and my full cleavage – I felt truly exposed. "What a pretty little catch I've got myself today;" he moved with slow, calculating steps until he stood before me – towering over my unguarded body.

Dropping to a kneeling position, he gripped my shoulders and pulled me upright, so I sat like a doll on a shelf in front of him, my legs outstretched, still bound tightly. He wriggled my feet out of my sandals and tossed them across the room. "Do you want me to remove your gag?" He trailed a single finger down my cheek and neck, tittering as I flinched. Eyes wide, with traces of smudged mascara printed under my lower lashes, I looked up at him with innocent desperation. I managed a fraction of a nod. "Are you going to be a quiet girl?" His wandering finger smoothed over my right breast, engorging my flinch into a jolt; a jolt that made my clit sizzle. Enjoying the response of my anxious body, he stroked my outer thigh, eliciting a succession of writhes and jerks as he established his authority over me. "If you want to be ungagged and untied, you're going to have to do better than that. Sit fucking still." His strokes contorted, increasing in ferocity, and his fingers sank into my inner thighs, nails drawing across my tender flesh.

"Please, please stop!" The words tasted foreign – barbed against my tongue. I didn't want him to stop. More than anything, I wanted him to continue. I fought the urge to beg and plead for Sir's fingers, desperately trying to stay in character. I needed to spread my legs and quickly came to hate the tether which kept them bound so tightly together. He knew what I needed – he sensed it; he smelled it. His paws moved up my tensed stomach, tearing another button from my blouse as it dangled loosely from its unravelled thread. His fingers forced their way into my bra, clawing a handful of breast and squeezing. He gripped and rolled my delicate nipple between his thumb and forefinger, staring into my wild eyes. With graduating intensity, he tightened his hold, morphing pleasure into pain and my performance into actuality. He tamed my thrashing with just a squeeze and a glare, locking his eyes onto mine and nodding approvingly as I began to comprehend the rules. "Please stop," I repeated earnestly, through my thick gag.

"Good girl… you're learning quickly." He released my nipple from its tortured hold and slapped my breast lightly. "If I want to touch you here," - he mauled both breasts over my clothing- "I can. And if I want to touch you here -" he raised the back of his hand to me and I squeezed my eyes closed, bracing for impact – "I fucking can!" but his fingers landed in a sensual glide, stroking my cheek instead. He chuckled, rubbing my bottom lip with his thumb as I peeked through half-opened eyes, body stiffened and still. "Every inch of this body is my property now. Do you understand, girl?" I nodded with as much sincerity as I could communicate without words.

Reaching into the back pocket of his jeans, he pulled out a palm-sized black and silver handle. I watched with trembling pleasure as he deftly flicked it open, revealing a short blade which glinted under the low light of the room; every fibre of my being fused and locked. Aside from the shallow puffs, which I allowed to exit through my nose, I remained completely silent and still. Straddling my restrained body, he gathered my loose, mussed hair into a ponytail and tilted my head backwards. His grip was uncharacteristically gentle but maybe it only felt that way because I was wholly focused on the grimacing blade which he brandished before me. My eyes tracked its steely shine as he pressed the flat edge against the swollen curve of my breast, edging it towards my cleavage. A soft, unexpected murmur fought against my gag as he increased the pressure – cold against the warmth of my supple flesh. My heart throbbed uncontrollably as he trailed the very tip of the knife across my shoulder and up my neck, towards my earlobe. It tickled and teased my skin, suspending me precariously between pleasure and unease. My stone-set features were sculpted from fear – I was so scared that the rapid pumping of my heart would jolt the knife and slice my tender skin. He rubbed the flat of the blade over my forehead and against my flustered cheek. The cold lifeless metal, a stark contrast to the heat that radiated from me, made me flinch and shudder. I squeezed my eyes shut.

"See how good you can be? Open your eyes and look at me." I hesitated, feeling the pointed tip of the blade resting against my quivering eyelashes. He wound my hair around his fist, keeping me so very still. I didn't need to wait for him to repeat himself – I slowly peeled apart my reluctant eyes, seeing the blur of hard steel sitting unnervingly close for comfort. I rolled my eyes upwards to meet his, managing to squeeze out a desperate plea. Pinching the layers of wrapped bondage tape, he sliced through with one sharp cut, pulling it from me, together with the sodden cloth. I breathed a long sigh of relief, stretching out my aching jaw and swallowing the spit that had pooled in my mouth.

"Thank you," I squeaked, hesitantly, offering my wrists to him for release. He flicked the blade back in on itself and returned it to his pocket, easing my nerves significantly.

"Good. Now, I'm going to untie you but you're going to fucking behave yourself." The brat within awoke at hearing his words… "You're going to strip down to your underwear – understood?" I pouted and glared up at him, refusing to answer, daring him to be firmer with me. He grabbed the Velcro strap that bound my wrists, tearing it apart with a piercing rip, before quickly repeating with the restraint around my ankles. I drew my knees to my chest, squeezing my arms around them and holding on tightly.

"I don't want to;" I spoke with quiet audacity, staring up into his impassive eyes as I waited for his reaction. I shuffled up against the wall, as though it may somehow help me to retract the words. He simply laughed – a hearty, menacing laugh that bounced around the four walls of my cell.

"Does it matter what you want?" I wanted to yell 'yes', to argue and taunt, but his movements distracted me. He proceeded across the room, reaching to the shelf above where the webcam was positioned. He pulled down the strap and repeated his question slowly, this time with an air of callousness; "Does it matter what you want?" Just seeing the thick, brown width of leather in his hand made my cunt pulse longingly and my mind race wickedly!

"I'm not taking my clothes off…" I tried to pull the flimsy fabric of my blouse back over my chest, knowing my efforts were in vain. "Fuck you," I said, awkwardly. I didn't like the feel of the words – I never swore at Sir and it felt so unnatural. I braced myself for his reaction as he smirked and shook his head – a concoction of excitement and repentance effervesced within my stomach.

He squeezed a hand around my neck, sliding my body up the wall as he forced me to my feet and pulled me from the mattress. I tried desperately to control my excitement, maintaining a persona of virtue and innocence, as I squirmed in his choking hold. "Take off your top, now," his tone remained collected and authoritative. My hands tugged at his; my fingers scratched lightly but to no effect.

"No! Fuck you!" I spat the words with greater conviction, enjoying the feel of his hands on my body and his control over my every action. I needed to be punished. He clocked the filthy gleam in my eyes and spun me around, pressing my body against the wall, holding me in place by the nape of my neck. I wriggled my arse, fingers splayed against the wall as I pushed and writhed in protest. With my skirt barely protecting my arse, he brought the strap down hard, spreading a stinging shock across both cheeks! He repeated the stroke a further three times, hitting the same spot every time, as to extract the loudest wail from my lungs! I rubbed my tender, glowing skin with the back of my hand, moaning and whimpering.

"Take your clothes off." He repeated his instruction, lowering his tone, whilst scooping my wrists away from my arse in one handful. He squeezed firmly, waiting for my reaction. Stubborn idiocy spilled from my lips, inviting six more strikes across my arse and thighs! He made sure I felt every, single one – the crack of leather against flesh sliced past my ears, mixing and mingling with my desperate cries. "Take your clothes off!" He rested the strap against my back, rubbing tauntingly. I looked deep within, wondering if I could muster enough reserves to handle a few more sharp slaps – just the thought doused my body in a cold sweat.

"No more! Okay, I'll take them off!" He released my wrists immediately, pulling me away from the wall and turning my shoulders to face him.

"Strip, fold your clothes, and hand them to me; you won't need them for a while." He leaned against the wall, getting ready to enjoy the show. My fingers trembled as I began to loosen the few remaining buttons down my sheer blouse. It fell open with ease, showcasing my breasts for Sir. I slipped my arms free and unzipped my skirt, pushing it over my hips and letting it fall to my ankles with a dull thud. Stepping out of my skirt, I turned away from Sir and bent at the waist to retrieve my clothes. I longed to see the look on his face as I pushed my arse out and arched my back, just my thin cotton knickers standing between his body and access to my wet, tight holes. To my disappointment, he didn't touch me. I hated how he could hold his composure better than me. I turned with my head bowed and handed him my neatly folded clothes. Catching sight of my stomach, my hands folded over my midriff, concealing my stretch marks. "Beautiful," he growled, circling my exposed body like a starved lion. "Now your underwear too and tie your hair back," he stroked the waistband of my panties, knowing they would reveal the extent of my arousal – they were embarrassingly soaked in my juices, giving him the upper-hand. Once he felt exactly how needy I was, I knew he would decide to tease me for longer. I unhooked my bra and let my heavy breasts spring free – my dark nipples pointed directly at him and did their best to invite the attention of his warm mouth.

"Even my... knickers?" I couldn't suppress my smirk as I scooped my hair high and secured it with the elastic I'd worn on my wrist. He tapped the strap against his palm impatiently, eyes narrowing as I peeled down the soft, damp fabric and released the sweet scent of my needy cunt into the space between us. I folded the sticky gusset inwards and placed the parcel into Sir's outstretched hand. He opened them flat and caressed with his thumb before deeply inhaling the intoxicating scent.

"Oh dear," he smeared my wetness over my lips, making me squirm and squeal. "Would a good girl really be this wet? And I haven't even touched you yet…" He grinned and squeezed my jaw, forcing my knickers into my mouth – forcing me to taste my neediness. I moaned and whimpered as he pushed every inch inside me, clamping his hand firmly over my lips. "I think you're going to make a good little fuck toy after all." He batted my hands back to my sides, slapping my face as to remind me of my position. "Hands on your head and don't you dare move a muscle." My arms trembled as I locked them just beneath my ponytail. He nudged my legs apart with his boot until I stood wide and exposed, eyes tracking and following him into my peripherals as he orbited slowly. "Tell me, why do you think you're here?" He pulled the knickers from my mouth and rubbed them against my spread cunt. I flinched but maintained my position, feeling him rub the material against my slit in deliberate, long strokes.

"I want to go home… please…" I whimpered, elbows bending inwards - he slapped my arse and I instantly pushed my chest back out.

"Oh, you are home, sweetheart. You're here to stay so you'd better get used to it." He shoved the knickers into his back pocket, working one finger from my swollen clit to my wet hole, examining his property. Spreading my dark lips to reveal my blushing pink wetness, he stared deep into my eyes and plunged his thick finger into my hole, curling forwards and locking my breath within the pit of my stomach. I did not dare to move.

"You can't touch me there!" I felt my heart rate rise as he bent his finger in a 'come hither' motion. I just knew that if he inserted a second finger and pumped for a few minutes, I would cum all over his hand with explosive ferocity but I also knew that he knew that too.

"Now that's where you're wrong," he chuckled, pushing knuckle deep inside me, making me squirm uncomfortably. "You are here for one reason and one reason only – you're here to please me." He must have felt my cunt contract and pulse around his finger as I weakened at hearing his words. I exhaled slowly, trying to maintain even a shred of control. He must have sensed I was waning; for without hesitation, he forced a second finger firmly inside me and pressed against the roughness of my g-spot, revelling as I leaked my juices around him, unable to contain myself. I felt myself rocking and grinding against the thick skin of his palm, further pleasuring myself without permission. I wondered, with bated breath, whether he would withdraw the delicious width that filled me. I didn't dare to look up into his eyes – I didn't want to know for sure. He increased the pressure but did not retreat. My hips rocked with hypnotic rhythm as I pulled myself closer and closer to satisfaction. My cunt sizzled as waves of pleasure rolled through my lower body. The heat between my legs radiated and burned from head to toe, clouding my mind and sheathing all prudence. And just as I reached the summit of ecstasy, he pulled the cord and plunged me into inert darkness. I longed to touch myself – to rub and rekindle the dwindling fire before it fizzled out completely. I looked Sir square in the eye – throwing out a dagger of anger and frustration as he slapped my mound gently, making me tingle in waves.

"You're here for my pleasure, Slut. You'll get yours after you've been a good girl. If you ever pleasure yourself without my permission again, you'll feel that strap against your disobedient little cunt." He smirked as I panted in long, shaky breaths, trying to centre myself. I hated how easily I had allowed myself to be played. "On your knees," he commanded, pressing on my shoulders until I knelt before him. He rubbed his thumb over my sulking lips and caressed my cheek in long, sensuous strokes. I desperately wanted to turn my head away – to shake off his touch. My eyebrows furrowed and my fists clenched - stubbornness beginning to consume my body and exasperation clouding my thoughts. With a smile curling the corner of his lower lip, he pushed his thumb into my mouth and massaged my tongue gently. "First, you're going to take my cock in your warm, wet little mouth." I opened my mouth and licked the back of his thumb, thawing ever so slightly. "You're going to give me a long, slow blowjob and you're going to take your fucking time, making sure you please me completely." I lifted my head, just enough to make eye contact, and tightened my lips to increase suction around the base of his thumb. "Have you ever sucked a cock before?" He gripped my ponytail and forced connection with my wild eyes, knowing his words would make my tummy flutter. I shook my head in innocent protest, keeping him between my lips until he pulled free and smeared my saliva over my wanton mouth.

"But, what if... I don't know how?" I loved the way he had to suppress a smile. I could almost see the wickedness playing in his mind – from Sunday morning blow jobs to back-seat quickies. He knew just how much I enjoyed feeling his thick length fill my mouth; he knew just how much pleasure it gave me to run my tongue along the thick vein that ran from base to sweet, pre-cum leaking, tip.

"I'll teach you exactly how I like it... don't you worry." He released my ponytail and spread his fingers, patting my hair, tenderly. I smiled and licked and twisted my mouth around his thumb, seeing the prominent bulge in his jeans. "Ohh, that's a good girl..." He fumbled with his fly, ready to release his throbbing cock. I started to suck harder, enjoying his impatience, moving my mouth up and down and grazing him gently with my teeth. "No teeth," he exhaled deeply, pushing boxers and jeans down slightly, cock springing free. I had to remind myself not to touch, even though he was stood to attention, ready for my mouth. He replaced his thumb with two fingers – making me taste the sweetness of my cunt: my tight, needy, desperate cunt. He had done that on purpose. I pulled away from his fingers and reached for his cock – taking exactly what I needed. "Not yet!" He spoke firmly, slapping my cheek and returning his fingers. He pushed against my tongue, making me gag. I hated being teased – I wanted his cock and I wanted it now. Without hesitation, I plunged forward and bit him sharply, causing him to jerk away! Teeth marks adorned his wet fingers – an alignment of deep, red indentations.

"Oops…" I assumed a low kneeling position, sucking on my lower lip and feigning an air of innocence. I braced myself for a slap to the cheek and a rough mouth fuck but he turned away, zipping up his jeans. He moved over to the shelves and a sense of apprehension weighed heavily in my gut; my heart rate began to intensify. "I'm sorry," I added, quickly – "I didn't mean to." His fingers hovered and twitched as he contemplated his selection.

"I know," he smiled kindly, making his final choice. My eyes widened as he pulled down the riding crop – it's thin, tapered end shrivelling the sass from my attitude. "You're going to be very, very sorry in twelve strikes time!" He whipped the leather-bound crop through the air, cracking down on the mattress beside me. I squealed and flinched, shaking my head!

"Please… please, no!" My stomach knotted at the thought of twelve, hard whacks. I shuffled back, swallowing the lump in my constricting throat, feeling my mouth dry up. I could barely take six strokes – how on earth could I handle twelve when I was already so sore? He was going to punish me – really punish me. Leaning the crop against the door frame, he pulled off the balaclava and ran his fingers through his static hair. He ordered me to my feet and reluctantly, I arose.

Wrapping a strong palm around the top of my arm - thumb pressing uncomfortably - he dragged me towards the door. Using his body to pin me in place, he pulled me onto the balls of my feet and bound my left wrist to the door-jam strap which was positioned above my head. How did I not notice this before? It was new – we had never played with this restraint before! My clit tingled. He continued, binding my right wrist and then pulling the strap incredibly tightly, securing both wrists together. I danced and wriggled, calves tensed, whining as he retrieved the crop and dragged it across the carpet until it stood by my side.

"Twelve thick, raised lines… then I stop." He trailed the end of the crop up the inside of my leg, leaning in to lick my neck, making me wince and shudder. I squeezed my eyes shut and exhaled a shaky, broken breath. He squeezed and mauled the tender flesh on my arse before moving his hand to my slender throat. "Bad girls need to be taught a lesson, don't they?"

I managed a whimper of agreement, feeling my insides churn.

He tightened his grip and pushed his fingers against my throat, drawing me higher, onto tiptoes.

"I'm sorry! Please..." I pressed my naked arse against his bulge in a feeble attempt to compel him.

"Please, SIR," he instructed. I nodded keenly and responded accordingly, so eager to appease. "Tell me why you are here, Slut. What is your job?" He loosened his hold and took a step back, rubbing the length of the crop against the centre of both cheeks.

"I'm here to please you, Sir-" with my back arched, like a curled leaf, I tensed my shoulders and spat out the words as loudly as I could manage, hoping for even an ounce of mercy.

"That's right. Now count out every stroke or I'll repeat it. Understood?" Tapping on my lower back, Sir pulled my arse into a raised position, ordering me to stay completely still. I nodded and turned to face away from him, preparing to feel the first stinging crack. He did not disappoint. I screamed out, louder than even he had anticipated; my arms jerked and yanked at the restraint with reflex action. I hated not being able to rub the sting away.

"One... Thank you, Sir." As soon as the words had exited my lips, he replaced the fading bite with another strike, of equal intensity. The sound of the crop making firm contact with my flesh made me wince more than the pain itself - the second spank felt manageable and I thanked Sir immediately. I held my composure through the third, fourth, fifth and even the sixth whack – I wanted to run my fingertips across my cheeks and feel the neat, raised lines, printed across the top half of my arse. As I pondered how red and pretty my decorated derriere would be, Sir caught me off guard and branded me with strike number seven. The tip of the crop wrapped around my squirming body and caught the top of my thigh, tearing a loud cry from my lungs. Pain seared across my arse and right thigh, making me curse stridently. He knew I was approaching my utmost limit so he stroked my cheek and let me rest against his chest for a second; the soft hairs on his torso absorbed the few, solitary tears which spilled from my lower lashes. "Seven. Thank you. Sir," I whispered, grateful to myself for remembering the words before Sir negated the strike.

"Are you ready to continue?" He lifted my chin and forced me to connect with his eyes. I couldn't respond with words – they remained wrapped around the lump in my throat – so I nodded. He placed me back in his hold, rubbing and examining my marked skin. His tenderness extracted more tears but I felt my heart rate return to a steady rhythm. "Tell me when you are ready. I hope you remember how many cracks you have left, my little pain slut." I felt my body heat as a wave of panic began to consume – did we get to seven or eight? Were we going to ten or twelve? The overwhelming pain of the last spank seemed to have dragged a hazy fog through my mind. I couldn't remember – would he really start again if I got it wrong? I had to remember but I just couldn't.

"I'm ready, Sir," I looked at him, apprehensively. I had to guess - four or five? Four. No, five… four… five… "F…five to go, Sir?" I squeezed my bottom lip between my teeth, waiting for confirmation.

"Good girl. Now, arse back in position – out as far as you can and the crop won't wrap." I obliged immediately, smirking as I dodged the bullet – tension drained through my nostrils as I exhaled deeply.

"Yes Sir," I smiled sweetly, gripping the restraints tightly around my fingers as I prepared myself. Time seemed to slow and stop as I waited for Sir. I tensed and tightened my stomach, legs beginning to ache from standing on the tips of my polished pink toes. He whipped the crop past my ear, chortling as I flinched, before choosing the location of the eighth welt and rubbing the crop from side to side. I squeezed my fists and accepted the whack with a simultaneous stream of tears; "thank you, Sir! Eight, thank you, Sir!" I sobbed the words, feeling strike number nine impact firmly! The tears wouldn't stop – they blurred my vision as the stinging pain misted thickly over any form of clarity.

"Arse out!" He barked, making me whimper and shake my head! My arse was throbbing; my skin alight. I couldn't do it. I struggled hard, begging him to stop, losing sense and focus. "Arse out, now," he repeated, insistently. His command filled my body with sheer desperation – I couldn't go on. "Use it, if you need to," he drew my eyes to his, centring my untamed panic, reminding me that I had my safe word. As the sting subsided and the fog lifted, I untangled my thoughts and put my needs into words:

"Red…Sir."

"Good girl." He put down the crop immediately and moved to my side.

Stinging hot tears flowed freely down my cheeks and neck, signifying the sheer rush and release of so much pent-up frustration. With my legs shaking, I was grateful to feel Sir's arm snake around my waist and support my weight as he untied me. He placed a kiss on my forehead and whispered to me that I had done well, before lowering me onto my knees. My heart swelled at hearing those words and I quickly wiped away my tears with the back of my hand. I winced as my heel pressed against the sore skin of my tender arse. I ran both hands over my burning hot flesh, feeling the tidy set of hard lines that Sir had gifted me.

"Open your mouth," he ordered. I smiled up at him as he undressed before me. I couldn't hide the excitement behind my eyes – taking in every part of his body as he revealed all that I desired, inch by beautiful inch. I longed to nestle against his strong chest and run my fingertips across his skin as I listened to the melody of his beating heart. I needed to touch his biceps and feel his strength as he pinned me down. He obliged to feed the hunger within, presenting me with his delicious length and gently brushing the glistening tip against my puckered lips.

"Tell me now, why are you here? What is your one purpose, my little slut?" He spoke with an air of darkness that taunted my cunt and lulled me deeper into depravity.

"I'm here to pleasure you, Sir..." my eyes projected the virtue of innocence but wickedness began to consume. I licked the end of his cock with caution, wondering if I should have asked permission. He settled my quandary instantaneously, encouraging his cock into my open mouth, telling me to please him – giving me licence to play and explore. I wrapped my palm around his thick length and swirled my tongue around his bell end - like it was a lollipop - savouring the saltiness of his pre-cum. My tongue travelled from base to tip, following the pulsing vein, making him groan with pleasure. His moans encouraged me to satisfy him further, taking him deeper into my warm, wet mouth and coating every inch with thick saliva.

"No hands, Sub" he murmured, falling out of role completely as my mouth drove him wild. I loved watching him lose himself, knowing I was having this effect on him. With my hands folded behind my back and my chest pushed out, he placed his palm beneath my ponytail and adjusted his position slowly, allowing himself to inch deeper into my mouth. Tongue out, drooling onto my breasts, I gagged around his cock and felt him hit the back of my throat. Coughing and moaning I resisted the urge to pull away, focusing on the taste of pre-cum down my throat and the look of ecstasy building in Sir's eyes. He thrust his length in and out of my open mouth, making my eyes water and mingle with the tears from my spanking. "Good. Girl," he grunted with each push. As he pulled out to let me catch my breath, long tendrils of saliva dragged across my chin. He slapped his meat against my cheek as I panted, wide-eyed, before thrusting deeper and holding me against his body, pubes ticking my nose and his balls against my chin. I rippled my tongue, knowing he was close; I longed to hear him growl for me. Pushing with arrhythmic action, he jerked and tightened his grip on my hair, releasing the deepest, guttural groan as he flooded my mouth and coated my throat, forcing me to swallow every drop of his offering, before I spilled it down my chin and made a mess of my face.

I panted hard, licking my lips and swallowing the remaining cum-laced saliva that filled my mouth. I reached for his gleaming cock, ready to lick him clean. Still moaning and recovering, he batted away my hand and pushed me backwards, onto the mattress. Without a second to enjoy basking in the afterglow of his orgasm, he grabbed the Velcro ties and rolled me onto my stomach, restraining my arms at the elbow and wrists. I struggled and fought him against him, feeling angry and confused. "Quiet down or you'll taste my belt," he hissed, binding my thighs and ankles equally as taut. Brushing my hair away from my forehead, he looked down at his hog-tied fuck-toy and grinned, satisfied with his handiwork. "I'll be back. Be fucking quiet or I'll gag and blindfold you as well. Got it?" I pouting and huffed, nodding my head, reluctantly. I glanced longingly towards him as he scooped up his clothes and exited the room. My heart sank as he slammed the door and locked it again behind him, leaving me alone, with only a sore arse and the taste of cum for company.

As I writhed, I felt the extent of my wetness between my thighs. I'd been so wholly focused on pleasing Sir, I hadn't realised just now needy my body had become. I rested my cheek against the mattress and relaxed my shoulders, as much as I could. The room felt so large and empty – I longed to be held close to Sir's chest and to listen to his heartbeat as he recovered. I could hear the sound of the shower running, through the sealed door, from down the hallway. My tired eyelids began to droop and my limbs began to wilt. I wondered what time it was and if he would return any time soon. I imagined being enveloped in tingling swirls of soapy steam; feeling cold tiles against my back and hot kisses against my lips. Darkness slouched over the fuzzy outline of the doorframe for longer and longer fragments of time until I finally succumbed and allowed my mind to enjoy the attention I so desperately longed for.

***

Soft, sensuous strokes… fingertips crossed my cheek and traced down my arm. I groaned, blinking and slowly stirring; stiffness had taken hold of my neck, making me moan with discomfort. "Wake up, sleepy slut – it's playtime." The room; the ties; the fantasy: it flooded back in an instant, rousing me from my slumber. I wiggled, revelling as I felt the delicious wetness of my cunt.

"Please untie me? I'll be such a good girl... I promise!" I squirmed, needing to stretch out; my voice was still gravelly after my nap. He rubbed my bruised arse with his rough palm - a subtle reminder of the punishment doled out to disobedient little brats. I couldn't help but smirk and I was grateful he couldn't see my face. As he untied my arms and legs, he squeezed and massaged away the stiffness and then sat me upright. As I wriggled beneath him, the scent of my sticky honeypot filled the room, leaving no doubt about what I needed from him.

"Lie on your back," he commanded. Sitting up on my knees, I rolled my shoulders and cracked my knuckles, stretching out a little before lying down, flat on my back. He gestured for me to spread my legs and I immediately obliged, revealing my tight hole and plump lips, all coated in my sweet juices. "Are you ready to play a game?" I swallowed hard, nervousness roiling within.

"Yes, Sir," I replied, automatically – voice lined with a tremble that definitely made his cock twitch. He picked up his mobile and moved to the end of the mattress, between my feet.

"Show me how you play with yourself when you're home alone and you think nobody is watching. Or when you're in an empty carpark…" He moved my right hand between my legs, encouraging me to rub my needy, swollen clit. I gasped softly.

"But… but I don't do things like that, Sir. I don't know what you think you saw." I chewed the inside of my lip, batting my eyelashes whilst slowly starting to take control of our circling fingers. "I'm a very good girl…" My words ignited his dominance, drawing his fingers from my cunt to my throat.

"That's right – you're going to be a fucking good girl and rub and finger that tight, wet little cunt until you are absolutely begging for permission to cum. Do you understand?" His grip had already sent my fingers into a wondrous frenzy and his words did nothing to stop my juices from leaking over the back of my hand. I honed my focus and concentrated on the zaps of pleasure, jolting from my sizzling clit. As I pushed one, and then two, fingers deep inside myself, I closed my eyes and squeezed and contracted, enjoying the pulsing sensations. "So sexy," he rasped, touching my knee and stroking in encouragement. A blood-red flash interrupted my sequence of jabs and strokes, like the sun appearing from behind an intermittent cloud when you are sunbathing. As I buried my fingers knuckle deep, a second flash shone against my closed lids, severing my concentration. As I looked up, Sir snapped another photograph, zooming in on my spread lips and swollen bud. "Don't stop. If you're going to stay, you'll need to earn your keep – I'll need some decent footage," as he spoke, he slapped my legs wide apart, keeping them open with his knees.

"Who will see them?" I pulled my fingers from my cunt and placed my hands over myself. Our pictures had always been for our eyes only – I wondered if he did want to post them online? The seed of curiosity began to sprout; "no faces?" I questioned, tentatively. I thirsted for attention and the notion of having random men and women watching me being naughty, and enjoying my body as much as Sir did, that really turned me on.

"If you behave, then maybe; if not, then maybe I'll have to share with a few people in your contacts." He lifted the phone higher and took a full-length photograph – from my wide, innocent eyes, to my D-Cup breasts, to the soft curls and smooth lips between my exposed thighs. "Look at these – look at the enjoyment on your face. You look very happy to be here," he chortled. The images were stunning – my body was surrounded in a serenity which I had never noticed or appreciated. For a moment, I could see myself through Sir's eyes. They made me want to please him even further. Reaching back, he retrieved my favourite pink jelly dildo and tossed it next to my stomach. "Now play with yourself, Slut," he shifted himself back into prime position and used the soft sternness of his gaze to draw my hand to the toy – he didn't need to utter even a word.

Wrapping my fingers around the thick, pliable shaft, I brought it to my mouth and sucked the end wet, before letting my spit dribble and coat it. Resting it against my pussy mound, I pushed forward, sliding over my desperate clit, spreading my lips and coating the shaft of the dildo in my sweet juices. Each flash of the camera encouraged me to play harder. I shuddered with pleasure as the veiny protrusions massaged and stimulated my sensitive nerve endings, sparking a concerto of quivers to gambol across my body. I looked directly into the lens, for a split second, before turning my attention back to my hungry cunt. I rubbed back and forth with ever-increasing ferocity; a series of long, breathy moans escaped my lips and filled the room, mixing and mingling with the scent of my wetness. As my body teetered on the edge of orgasm, I plunged the dildo inside my cunt; writhing and grinding - hips raised – I felt a desperate need to burst ablaze.

"Please, Sir…" I swapped hands, trying to hold myself on the pinnacle, continuing to pump and rub and rub and pump. "Please, Sir!" With sheer desperation in my voice, I pleaded for permission.

"Please what? Use your words;" he was ready to video me cumming.

"Please let me cum, please Sir, I beg you!" Body laced with a thin veil of sweat, I panted and pushed away from the mattress, feeling my cunt drip with neediness.

"Good girl. Yes, cum hard for me," he groaned with satisfaction, as I finally let go and let out a cry of pure ecstasy. Holding the dildo against my pussy wall and squeezing around it, I brought myself to orgasm, thrusting in and out, and sending seismic tremor after tremor rippling through every inch of my body. As I finally settled - dildo still buried inside me – he pulled it out with a wet 'pop' and gently rubbed it over my sensitive bud, enjoying watching me flinch and gasp from the aftershocks.

"That was so fucking beautiful. I think you'll enjoy watching that back later." He stroked my forehead, making me beam with pride. I wanted to say, 'thank you, Sir,' but my brain couldn't put the thought into action. I was still trying to catch my breath. I moved over, waiting for him to join me but he was firmly back in character. I loved how horny he was – I was sure I wouldn't get any recovery time! "You've definitely done that before, haven't you?" The coyness in my eyes could have fooled some if it wasn't for the smirk plastered visibly across my face. "What else have you done before? Has that tight little cunt been fucked?" He traced his fingers across my stomach and gently slapped my spread pussy, making me groan. "Of course it has," he laughed, licking his fingers. "What about your other hole?" I whimpered, shaking my head and squeezing my thighs closed.

"No Sir, never! You can't... it's too tight!" as I shuffled back, he yanked me back in place by my ankles, encouraging my legs open with a few sharp slaps.

"That sounds like a challenge, Slut," he rubbed and circled my arse hole, slowly increasing the pressure, before plunging a thick finger knuckle-deep. My groaning and contorting only fuelled his appetite. "Remind me – why are you fucking here?"

"To please you," I responded with impudence, rolling my eyes away from his with a huff. Lifting my legs onto his shoulders, he ordered me to spread my cheeks, placing my hands in position and pulling wide. His eyes glimmered with dark desire as my tight arse hole winked back at him. I gasped as he squeezed cold lube directly between my cheeks, rubbing crudely before coating his thick cock. As he leaned forward and nudged his tip against my hole, I couldn't help but whimper and tense my body. I felt my heartbeat resonate in my ears.

"Just relax…" he cooed, trying again with just the end. Taking in a deep, shaky breath through my nose, I concentrated on not squeezing my hole, feeling Sir open me gently and then pause. "Good girl," he stroked my ankle and kissed my calf; "ready for more?"

"Slowly Sir, please!" With our eyes locked together, he pushed gently, only stopping when I signalled it was too much. My gasps melted into sensuous groans as he fed me inch after inch until he was buried fully inside of me. Leaning in, he gripped my wrists and pinned them over my head, pushing deeper still, as to make me cry out! I tugged firmly but his strength was insurmountable, sparking defiance within. The harder I struggled, the tighter he gripped me, and the tighter he held me, the more I enjoyed giving him a reason to restrain me! As he thrust and stretched me, I revelled in feeling helpless beneath him. The world had faded into insignificance and all that remained was a pool of pleasure and pain, into which Sir rhythmically and relentlessly pushed and plunged me, forcing me to relish being beneath the surface.

"So fucking tight," he growled, squeezing my throat and holding me still. I sucked in rasps of air, moaning as each lunge shoved me further and further backwards until my head was no longer on the mattress. "On all fours, arse up," he commanded, pulling me back by my ankles and flipping me onto my stomach. Without warning, he squeezed handfuls of my sore, marked arse and thrust his cock fully inside me! I screamed out, hungry for more, which Sir provided - spanking my cheeks in time with every delicious thrust. I pushed my arse back to meet his efforts; the slap of clammy, sex-coated skin colliding, filled the room. "I'm going to cum inside you, Sub," he said, between short pants. I nodded - too consumed to respond - nails scrapping the mattress as I rolled my arse up and down his length, ready to milk him dry. "Ohh, that's so good! Don't stop!" He pulled me back against him and mirrored my movements, helping me to keep pace. Getting closer and closer, he pushed harder until my legs trembled and I flattened beneath him. Wrapping a hand around my mouth, he gagged my screams and restrained my flailing limbs, squirting jet after jet of hot cum, deep inside me! I gasped and moaned into the mattress as he collapsed on top of me and kissed my neck, exhaling slowly as he recovered.

Sitting up, he smiled down at me as I rolled over to look at him. I always felt deliciously mischievous, having Sir's cum in my arse, and the look on my face showed him just how much I had needed it. "Do you want to keep it inside of you?" He reached across to where the lube was discarded and grabbed my glass butt plug from the wash bag, waiting for my decision. I never usually did but today, I wanted to. I nodded eagerly and turned to my side, facing away from him, so he could plug me. It slid in with ease and settled snugly; I tightened and squeezed around it, hoping it would stay nestled inside of me. Each contraction reminded me of the pounding I had just received, warming me with contentment. I loved the feeling. As I turned back, Sir stood up; he had the key in his hand, making my heart sink immediately.

"Wait, Sir! Please don't leave," I whimpered, my eyes filling at the thought of being alone.

"I'm not leaving; I just need to freshen up," he knelt and kissed my mussed hair, reaching between my legs. "I'll be ready for your sweet little cunt soon, Sub," he smiled, rubbing my wetness and gently pushing a finger inside me. My panic subsided. Awash with relief and adoration, I agreed eagerly and watched in anticipation as he walked towards the door. He unlocked it, leaving the key in place and the door ajar. The sound of running water, from down the hallway, set my heart thumping with excitement – he would be back soon. I untangled my hair bobble and made an effort to run my fingers through my tangled, matted tresses, scooping and twisting my hair into a high bun. I wondered what I must look like right now. Usually, it would have bothered me but I really didn't care tonight. I could see how much Sir wanted me – just as badly as I needed him – and that was enough.

I lay back and watched the dancing shadows on the ceiling as I played back through the last few hours. I stroked my forearm, feeling where I would have a pretty little bruise this time tomorrow. My hand moved across my sore, aching breasts, down my stiff body, resting against my pubic mound. A shuffle and creak diverted my attention to the doorway. Sir was standing there, leaning against the frame, watching and smiling. "How long have you been there?" I laughed, realising I was drifting in my own world.

"Long enough," he responded, wandering over. "Want to come to bed?" The thought of lifting my exhausted body and dragging my sore bones three feet down the hallway was too much. I shook my head and shuffled towards the wall. He rolled his eyes at my laziness before softening into a smile and lying down beside me.

"Thank you, Sir," I leaned in and kissed his lips. I'd really missed that tonight. I rolled onto my elbows and kissed him again, fully and deeply this time. "Thank you so, so fucking much, Sir. It was better than I ever imagined." I injected my gratitude into my kisses, my tongue gliding over his as I moved to straddle him.

"You were very, very good, Sub." His hands snaked over my body, groping my most tender parts, looking for groans and winces. He grinned as I delivered in abundance! Leaning forward and pressing my breasts against his chest, I kissed him deeply and tugged his lower lip between my teeth, my nails grazing his skin lightly. Mouths locked, he flipped me beneath his body with absolute ease and pinned my hands beside my ears, fingers intertwined. Holding our bodies together as one, he carefully pushed his throbbing length inside my pussy, drawing a deep moan of utter satisfaction from my lips.

"Yes, Sir - fuck me hard, please!" My eyes invited him to unleash his dominance upon me. Feeling the strength and weight of his body upon me reminded me of the security that came from my submission to him. I wrapped my legs around him and felt him plunge further inside me still, using pure animalistic force and releasing his most carnal desires. He kissed and nibbled my lips and neck and nipples, holding me firmly under his body with every delicious grunt. Hips rocking, he slowed to a steady pace.

"Where do you want my cum, Sub?" He released my hands and I wrapped my arms around his neck, stroking the back of his hair.

"Over my breasts, Sir. Please," I panted — a filthy glint in my eye. Nodding, he pulled out and moved to straddle my body, working his shaft furiously as I whispered filthy words and tried to coax him to fruition. I licked my lips as the lustful words left my mouth and swirled playfully around his senses, pushing him closer and closer to orgasm. I squeezed my breasts together as he squirted warm salty cum over my neck and between my cleavage. A smile spread across my face and I propped myself up, just enough to lick his cock clean. He gasped and jolted, leaking the last drops directly onto my tongue.

As I settled my head onto Sir's chest, listening to the steady rhythm of his drumming heart, he wrapped his arms around my body, holding me securely and gently caressing my skin. "I guess we should go to bed, Sir?" I mumbled, eyes heavy; the room quickly fading around me. Blotches of burnt orange and auburn swirled before my eyes and a ripple of anticipation washed over me. The drumming tailed off into a distant corner of my mind, replaced by the sound of crunching sand and gravel. As I blinked sleepily, the silver crescent of the moon appeared from behind a smudge of cloud, casting a cool light over my naked body and black stiletto sandals.

"You just close your eyes, Sub, I'll take care of that."

As I entered the secluded carpark and scanned the towering hedges around the perimeter, Sir's voice whispered into my ear; "have sweet and filthy dreams, Sub."

Thank you so much for taking the time to read Nisha's Taste of Submission; I hope you thoroughly enjoyed! If so, please will you take the time to kindly leave a small review on? It would be much appreciated.

Need more steamy erotica? Check out the other books in the *A Taste of Submission* series.

www.ingramcontent.com/pod-product-compliance
Lightning Source LLC
LaVergne TN
LVHW092313040225
802993LV00027B/302